Daddy's Taboo Secrets

Volume 2: The Boss's Obsession

Written by Caressa Pink

Steam Heat Press

The stories and art contained herein are the intellectual property of the individual author. No duplication may be made without the explicit consent of that author.
All written work is the property of Caressa Pink.

CONTENTS

Chapter One

We were in public, but I didn't care.

No, that's a lie. I cared a *lot*.

All of the seats in the Metro car were taken, so Mr. Brig and I had to stand.

Very close together.

And with his chest pressed against my back, no one could see his crotch.

And only I could feel it.

Dinner had been an agonizingly, wonderfully slow build-up to the train ride back to my UCLA dorm room. The sights, smells, and tastes had melted into a dreamlike, hazy memory of wanting my boyfriend to whisk me out of the restaurant and turn me into dessert.

Of course, by the end of the meal, I was ready to be eaten right then and there.

In front of everybody.

Which brought us to the train.

Undoubtedly, most people didn't realize that the dignified, Brioni-clad Harrison Brig was my boyfriend.

Sharply dressed, well-spoken, authoritative without being commanding, there was no doubt that the physically fit 45-year-old man could have dated anyone he deemed worthy.

And no one would have suspected that choice would be me.

At only eighteen, most people would dismiss me as more of a little girl than a woman. Too emotional. Too bratty.

And way too unsure of what she wants.

I can promise that one of those things is wrong.

Neither Harrison nor I had doubted what we wanted the entire night. His hands sliding gently through my hair. The way his strong, firm fingertips rolled across my soft hands. The look in his eyes when were gawking at each other without words, as I watched his internal demons fight over whether he wanted to nourish and protect me more than he wanted to conquer and own me.

He wanted them both as much as I did.

There was no way to hide that fact when his crotch was pushed so firmly against my back. We were, doubtlessly, going to need these outfits dry-cleaned, given the mark that Harrison was currently leaving on them.

A warm blossom of adrenaline spread through my chest as I realized how badly Mr. Brig wanted me there and then, and how hard he was forcing himself to stay restrained.

I decided to make things harder.

I leaned my light frame against his sturdy one, melting my soft back into his torso. Even through the Brioni suit, I could feel the firm contours of his abs and pecs.

Those were nothing, of course, when compared with the contours of what lay just below.

I'd chosen my sexiest, most uncomfortable heels for the night, but I was still hopelessly diminutive next to my boyfriend. The top of my head was just high enough to nestle against his chin, and his dick fit snugly into the curvature of my lower back.

I pushed so hard that he had to grab the rails for support.

Then I rubbed.

I started slowly, lifting myself up and down, sliding my silky dress against his unyielding cock.

The first moan was soft enough so that only I understood what was happening.

I moved faster. Just an inch at a time, subtle enough to go unnoticed by the multitude of passengers around us.

Probably.

I pushed harder still, nearly tumbling out of my heels as he grabbed the rail with his other hand for support.

The woman on the seat next to us raised an eyebrow as he moaned audibly.

"Lily," he whispered. "Stop it. Behave yourself."

I turned my head around and lightly kissed his neck, followed with the tiniest of bites.

I slid down.

Then he grabbed me by the shoulders and physically pushed me away. I was taken aback by just how little effort it took for him to manhandle my entire body.

I realized in that instant just how easily he could physically control me if he so desired. The thought caused my head to spin, and for the first time I noticed how wet the crotch of my panties had gotten. They were uncomfortably damp; for a wild moment, I imagined sliding them off in front of everyone and pressing them into Harrison's hands while the crowd watched.

More dampness.

I moved to lean back against Mr. Brig, but he grabbed my arms and held me firmly in place.

"Lily," he whispered, louder this time, "I am asking you to be *obedient*."

I tried to resist his grasp, but he was unyielding. Then I attempted to reach behind me and find his crotch with my fingertips. But it quickly became apparent that he would effortlessly win any contest of physical strength, so I acquiesced to his control. I leaned back so that my hair would brush softly against his neck. "Yes, sir," I cooed, prompting the nearby woman to raise her other eyebrow.

I fought *just* softly enough so that he was forced to restrain me for the rest of the journey.

It was impossible to resist staring at Mr. Brig in adoration, so I had long ago stopped trying. I allowed my eyes a decadent feast that would pulse downward to whet the appetite between my thighs.

So when I caught *him* gawking at something that wasn't *me*, unexpected jealousy nearly forced a scream from my throat.

Nearly.

Instead, I opted for the mature approach.

"I see you found something sexier to ogle, hmm?" I pouted.

He looked down at me, smiled, and nodded. An icy chill grabbed my chest.

"Look," he said, pointing across the street. "It's a Jaguar XJ220. You will *not* see them often."

The car was, admittedly, shiny and pretty. But I was distracted by the sudden notion of Mr. Brig ogling another woman as he spread her open. Conflicting emotions of jealousy and unexpected arousal swirled in my head, and for a moment I realized just how little I knew myself.

"I know that Nolan Radner has one of those. He's one of the country's foremost Jaguar collectors. He lives right here in Westwood."

I tried to focus on what he was saying, but found it difficult. "He's a friend of yours?"

Harrison laughed, and I felt childish. "No, we've never crossed paths. I'd give just about anything to spend an afternoon in his garage, though."

We walked on in silence. I was irritated at him for laughing, and I was irritated at myself for realizing how enticed I was by the thought of *secretly* watching him while he took another woman. I was jealous of her, despite the fact that she didn't exist, and I didn't know how to voice my frustration when I didn't understand it myself.

"Wait," Mr. Brig interjected, stopping me and lifting up my chin with one gentle finger. He studied my expression with academic intensity.

Then his face shifted with a sudden moment of understanding. "Lily, I laughed at you, and I am sorry. It was wrong of me." He bent down and kissed me softly. "You know I only ever want to make you smile," he whispered in the chocolaty baritone that made my spine and neck tingle warmly.

The pleasant sensation flowed through my head, and I quickly forgot why I'd been mad. Despite all weak efforts, I couldn't hide how successful his last sentence really was.

"Well, Mr. Brig," I offered coyly, "why are we standing here, then? I believe you said that you wanted to explore someone's garage."

"This is your father?" asked the bored girl behind the desk.

We were checking in before entering my dorm room, and every guest had to register.

"Um," Harrison responded awkwardly, redness creeping up his face.

To be honest, I loved seeing him speechless, because it was so rare. So much lurked below his surface that he could easily slip into any conversation and prove himself a kindly master of whatever topic he chose.

Knowing that *I* could affect him thrilled me.

I slipped my hand into his. "Yep, that's right." I looked up at him in adoration. "Come walk me to my room and tuck me into bed."

I could feel the desk girl staring as I pulled Mr. Brig down the hall.

"You're *sure* that both roommates will be gone for the weekend?" Harrison asked nervously as we walked briskly to my door. "Lily, I haven't been-" he stared at me with a mixture of apprehension and longing "-*active* in a college dorm room for over twenty years."

I stopped by the door, leaned against the wall, then pulled him close. I stared up at him with awe, respect, lust, and at hint of fear.

Then I grabbed his necktie.

The kiss was frantic, and that made it perfect. I didn't want people to stare – but I *did* want that, too. I couldn't wait to rush inside, but didn't want the moment to end. He was torn and I wanted to be torn, so the urgent forcing of my lips upon his was anxious, unplanned, and fleeting.

The best kisses are filled with the nervous fear that the moment cannot last.

Without breaking eye contact, I opened my door, pulled him inside, then locked it behind us.

"Do people still… put neckties on the knob?" Harrison asked nervously. He sighed. "I certainly never thought I'd have to deal with this again." He ran his fingers through his hair, lightly brushing the graying wisps around his temples. The soft signs of aging, while often judged as undesirable, made me weak for a man who had clearly known so much of the world.

He held back as I pulled him forward by his tie. "You know how I *love* seeing you wear this, Mr. Brig." I stood on my toes as I pulled him down close enough for us to kiss once more.

Then I leaned against his cheek and lightly traced the tip of my tongue along the edge of his ear. "I'm sorry if I was a disobedient little girl on the train, Mr. Brig. But I love testing your limits."

The dam broke.

He grabbed both my wrists and pushed me back against the wall. He made no pretense of hiding his erection now as he pressed it aggressively against my stomach. I squirmed beneath his grasp, but he just squeezed me tighter. I looked deeply into his stormcloud gray eyes; where there once had been conflict between desire and restraint, I now saw only hunger. It terrified me to realize how insatiable his craving had become, and it thrilled me to know that his appetite was only for me.

Unable to move my arms, I pushed my stomach against his slim, supple waist, knowing that it would provoke an already fearsome carnal drive.

He moaned.

Then Mr. Brig dropped my arms, grabbed my ass, and easily lifted me off the ground. He kissed and bit my neck, my cheek, my ear.

Then he tossed me onto the bed like a rag doll.

He pulled the top of my dress down, suddenly exposing my nipple. I felt bare and chilly.

"Mr. Brig, if you want to take of my dress, lift it from bel-" He cut off my voice by pressing a hand against my mouth, and I understood that he would be taking what he wanted from me as he saw fit.

I closed my eyes as he lowered his mouth onto my nipple.

Every nerve around my breast radiated an itchy, electric alarm. I struggled to breathe as he sucked me inward, spinning my head wildly.

Then he bit.

I felt a level of sensitivity that didn't know existed. *How* could one nipple be so vulnerable?

Then he rolled his tongue across it.

I whimpered. The sensation was too much for just foreplay.

So I grabbed his head and pulled it closer to my chest, wrapping my legs around his torso so that the tips of my heels touched each other, and lifted my hips up into him.

He reached around and unfastened my legs, causing me to fall lightly onto the bed.

I whined. "Why won't you let me touch you, Mr. Brig?" I breathed.

He pressed his hand against my lips. "I'll touch you as I please, Lily," he ordered firmly, "but I expect patience from you in return."

I wanted to pout about how unfair that was. Instead, I pulled one of his fingers into my mouth, closed my eyes, and sucked.

I could feel his resolve melting. So I flitted my tongue across his finger. Two could play at the teasing game, and I was so horny at this point that I was content to have any part of his body inside me.

I rested my teeth on his skin, looked up at him, then grazed the edges of my teeth ever so lightly along the shaft of his finger.

He gasped.

I felt his weakness – I *tasted* it – and consumed it greedily. I took the entirety of his finger into my mouth, then slowly drew back, leaving a light sheen of wetness in my wake. I looked up at him, wide-eyed, and, pulled the finger inside me once more. My tongue acted of its own accord, gently caressing the underside of his digit before coiling and uncoiling itself around his flesh.

Mr. Brig was breathing so fast that he sounded ready to faint.

So I lifted my hand and gently stroked my fingertips against the underside of his palm.

The next sequence of events flowed quickly beyond my control. He reached back, popped off my heels, then stood me up on the floor. He hopped off the bed and pulled the dress down past my breasts, over my stomach, and down to my ass. His efforts finally met resistance as he attempted to pull the garment past my posterior; and, when the dress refused to do his bidding, he yanked it hard enough to cause an audible tear.

Now that I was reduced to nothing but a bra and thoroughly soaked panties, he threw me back onto the bed. He kicked off his own shoes and tossed his jacket hastily to the floor, but remained otherwise clothed.

Then he hopped onto the bed and stalked toward me like a great cat.

For a moment, I was terrified.

It felt wonderful.

He slid one hand slid under the front of my bra. Before I even realized that he'd been reaching for the clasp, Mr. Brig had opened it with smooth skill. It unfolded, exposing my left breast entirely while my right nipple peeked from behind the edge.

He grazed my side with his soft, strong hands, causing me to shudder as he tickled my exposed ribs. Mr. Brig brushed the bra aside, then paused to stare down in awe at my exposed chest.

I had seen that same look on his face when the Norton Simon Museum hosted a Van Gogh exhibit three weeks before. He had gazed with such all-encompassing wonder that he forgot to close his mouth. I asked Mr. Brig how it made him feel, and he laughed. He said that wasn't the question *most* people asked when they had to fake an understanding of things he liked, and that was one of the reasons he loved me. He kissed me then, and told me that he is overwhelmed in front of beauty so sublime that he loses all sense of self in its raw perfection.

He stared at my chest like this now. It made me feel vulgar and beautiful at the same time, and that's one of the *many* reasons I loved him.

I remained still as he slid his fingers over my breasts, teasing both nipples at the same time before grasping them. Slowly, he straddled my bare torso, forcing me down and pinning my arms to my sides.

Then he pulled.

Mr. Brig softly lifted and stretched my breasts. My initial reaction was to move my arms, but I found myself unable to budge beneath him.

He was going to play with my tits as he saw fit, and I was powerless to stop him.

That thought alone nearly sent me over the edge. "Please," I whispered.

"Please *what*, little girl?"

My breaths were coming in short gasps. "Please, just touch my clit. Graze it. Flick it. *Any*thing, you just need to touch it and I'll cum, then you can do anything you want to the rest of my body."

He smiled and dropped one nipple, reaching back to stroke my inner thigh. "Silly girl, I'll do anything I want to your body regardless of what I choose to do with your clit." His finger crept *slowly* toward the edge of my crotch. "You're a wonderful treat, Lily, but you can be *so* hard to control sometimes." He spread his fingers so than another digit brushed along the opposite inner thigh.

With a sudden lurch, I pulled on hand free from his leg. I sat halfway up and reached around his body, inches away from stroking my own pussy and releasing the tension that had been building since dinner.

But he expertly caught my wrist and pinned it to the mattress next to my head. I let out a low scream. He smiled as he stared down at my tits, which were now jiggling uncontrollably as I panted for air after my physical exertion.

He smiled, then bent down to kiss my stomach. Slowly, he dragged the tip of his tongue across my abs. He paused to kiss my navel. Then he ran his tongue down further, kissing the skin at the edge of my blue cotton panties.

He moved to the inside of my right thigh. *This is it*, I thought. *I'm going to cum*. He dove into the crook of my hips, kissing the sensitive skin.

And he stayed there.

Mr. Brig ate the inside of my thigh with the same intensity that I craved two inches to the left. His tongue danced across my inner thigh in *just* the perfect way that my clit screamed for.

I pulled my other arm free, grabbed his salt-and-pepper hair, and tried to force his face onto my clit.

His neck was far too strong for me, and he showed no outward effort in successfully resisting my attempts. I let out another low scream of frustration.

So he lifted his head and moved it across my crotch.

Too *far* across my crotch.

I realized in agony that he was going to eat me out on the wrong side once again.

Just to frustrate me.

He kissed my skin, and I thrust my waist aggressively in response.

He grunted and leapt on top of me, his face stopping half an inch from mine. We were both panting, both trying to control the other but unable to master ourselves, both defined by a lust so powerful that it rendered us afraid of who we truly were.

"Kiss me, eat me, fuck me, or spank me, Mr. Brig, I don't care. I need to *feel* your effect on my body, and I need it *now*."

He paused.

Then he lifted my hips and slipped my panties over my ass, up my thighs, and past my feet. He quickly stuffed them inside my mouth, overwhelming me with the flavor of my own pussy. It was shameful and gratifying all at once.

Then he dove toward my slit, hovering his face just in front of it, and slowly spread it with his fingers.

He lowered his tongue to the base of my pussy, then stroked my asshole with his finger. The thrill was so sudden that I bucked my hips.

"Calm down, little Lily, if you want me inside of you."

I closed my eyes and tried to control my breathing.

He touched my outer lips with his tongue, allowing my juice and his drool to lazily intermingle. He stroked my asshole again; controlling the sudden shock was like attempting to restrain a knee-jerk reaction beneath a doctor's mallet.

"Hold still," he whispered.

Then he grazed his tongue along my inner lips. My heart raced so fast that I felt ready to spring out of bed, run a few laps around the building, then come back to organize my dorm room while simultaneously getting fucked from behind.

But I waited.

When his tongue finally, finally, *finally* found my clit, he gave it the tiniest flick.

I gasped.

Then he drew a longer graze of his tongue.

I groaned.

Then he gave a strong, firm, deliberate tongue stroke across my clit that melted me. I made no attempt to hide my moan as it grew into a slightly muffled shriek.

Unable to restrain myself, I wheeled around and pinned him to the bed. Then I straddled his head and pressed my pussy down, hard, onto his face. "Eat my cunt, you fucking tease, *eat it now*."

I was sure that he would reject me.

But he gave in. Harrison pulled my lips into his mouth, drinking deeply as though determined to leave me dry. He licked my clit furiously, and I responded by grinding my crotch *hard* against his face. I distantly wondered if he was going to drown in my pussy juice, but was too overwhelmed to control myself. I was about to cum, and I needed him to consume every drop of what he had created.

I bit my lip. This was going to be a big one.

The door burst open, and my roommate, Emma, walked in. "Lily, are you okay? I thought I heard you yell-"

I looked up at her in shock, completely frozen. She stared back at me, stark naked and riding my boyfriend's face like a mechanical bull.

Her face flushed red and she grinned. "Oh. Looks like everything's under control." Her eyes lingered on Harrison a moment longer before she turned around and walked toward the exit.

"You know," she offered while pulling the door closed, "you really should have put a necktie on the knob."

She shut it with a soft click.

I was equally mortified and horny. Looking down at Harrison's crotch, I could see that his pants were still sporting a full circus tent. What were we supposed to do?

I peeled myself off of his face and wrapped the covers around me, waiting for his comforting embrace.

It didn't come.

Slowly, he sat up.

Then he slid off the bed, pulled on his shoes, and wrapped the jacket around him.

Comfort me, screamed the voice in my head. *Tell me that you're not ashamed of me. I know you're not, but I need to hear it sometimes, especially right now.* I pulled my legs close and buried my head in my knees. *Neither of us did anything wrong, but sometimes I feel like you think I'm not right. I know it doesn't make any sense, but I just need you to say the right thing in the wrong moment. Please, just understand that.*

My thoughts were very articulate. But I didn't know how to say them, so I remained silent.

"Lily, this was a mistake. The wrong public image will cost me my job." Harrison sighed. "I don't belong in a dorm room." He leaned over, pulled my shoulder close, and kissed me on the top of my head. I pulled the blankets tighter.

We paused.

Then, "I should go." He walked toward the door.

Wait, the voice in my head called as he stepped over the threshold and snapped it shut behind him.

Please, just say that you belong with me.

Chapter Two

"And that's when he left," I heaved softly, leaning back in my chair.

Carmen ran her fingers softly through my hair, lifting a lock. She pulled firmly, picking up the thread of a new braid. The contrast between gentle caressing and tight binding relaxed my scalp as she worked.

She cast her eyes downward, made eye contact with my reflection, and smiled sadly. "Girl, you have had one hell of a first semester."

I nodded slightly, but her fingers restrained most of my head movement. "It's hard," I sighed. "Pretty much no one can understand my boyfriend... issues. Even if my mom approved of me dating the man who was my dad's best friend when he was alive-"

"Fucking the man," Carmen smirked. "She's probably most uncomfortable with you *fucking* a man who's old enough to be your dad." She slid her fingers along another strand of hair, holding it loosely before pulling taut once more.

I grinned. "You're vulgar."

She raised an eyebrow. "I'm accurate." Carmen shrugged. "Besides, you like it. It turns out that sweet, innocent Lily *is* vulgar, just like the rest of us."

I watched my face turn red in the mirror. "Anyway, the last thing my mom wants to hear is a description about my date with Harrison. She hasn't been with any man in five years, and says that Annalise is the best thing that ever happened to her."

Carmen's reflection smiled, but she remained focused on the manual task at hand.

I sighed again. The tension flowed out of me as she continued to play with my hair. "Obviously, I can't talk with my roommate about it. Emma came right in the middle of things, and I'm too mortified to look at her." My skin grew hot. "I mean, she saw *everything* - my chest was facing the door, and Harrison's tongue was inside my-"

I cut myself off, unable to go further.

"Lily, people would line up to see your body. You have *nothing* to be ashamed of," Carmen insisted.

I swallowed. "I... can't help it. I feel vulgar sometimes, and Harrison makes me so *vulnerable*."

She rested her hands on my temples, then turned my head around to face hers. "Lily, this is important: did Emma get to see your boyfriend's dick?"

I grinned despite myself, gave her arm a sharp but playful slap, then snapped my head back to face the mirror. "Don't be weird, Carmen. And no, he still had his pants on."

She sighed. "Sucks for Emma."

"Sucks for *me*," I shot back.

"It sounds like you didn't get to suck anything," she retorted.

My shoulders slumped. "I gave a blowjob to his finger. That's it."

She pulled on my hair, forcing me to look up at her. "His *finger?* You're into some wild shit." She giggled. "I like it."

"I didn't *mean* to do the finger thing. I – I don't know how to explain it."

Carmen shrugged. "You got caught up in the moment and discovered something about yourself that had been hidden until the right person had the key to unlock you."

I squirmed, not knowing what to say.

Because she was exactly right, and I hadn't realized what I was feeling until she came along and articulated it perfectly.

"But you're still frustrated, because what you really wanted was that cock down your throat where it belongs."

My entire body flushed this time, and I slapped her a little harder than before.

"Ow! Damn, girl, no wonder he spanked you hard enough to leave a bruise!"

I covered my face with my hands. Carmen dropped the current strand of hair, knelt down in front of me, and pulled my wrists back. I resisted fruitlessly as she gave intense eye contact.

"Listen, Lily," she explained softly. "Girls spent their lives being taught that our desires are shameful, disgusting, and bad. Don't resist the part of you that embraces your basic needs." She smiled sadly. "If Harrison is yours, then *own* that fact without any shame."

I wiped away a tear. "I'm *always* afraid of losing him, Carmen. It feels like the world is determined to pull him away from me, and it won't stop until the only man I've ever loved is gone."

She stood up, pulled me next to her, and hugged me tightly. I could feel the tension draining more, and I unsuccessfully fought the first teardrops and they melted into her strawberry-scented hair.

"Lily," she pressed, moving my face inches in front of her own, "what can you give him that no one else can?"

"You can't come inside," the bored security guard responded offhandedly.

I stared at him in shock, not knowing what to say. "But – my boyfriend works here. I wanted to surprise him at his office," I explained nervously.

He raised an eyebrow. "Your *boyfriend* works here. Of course." The man looked me up and down. I suddenly felt very self-conscious in my bright sundress, braided hair, and Vans. He sighed. "Look, Miss, the Brig Corporation doesn't have any high school or college kids working here that I'm aware of. You've got the wrong building."

My eyes got itchy, but I forced myself to stay calm. "I *am* at the right place. Harrison Brig is my boyfriend."

He smiled condescendingly. "Okay, Miss, you've wasted enough of my time. Please leave the premises. I'm not going to ask you again."

My hands started shaking, so I folded them tightly. "Please call Mr. Brig's office. He'll come down and get me," I responded in a much meeker voice than I had intended.

"No," he answered flatly.

All of my instincts told me to back away.

Instead, I confidently walked past him.

"Miss!" he shouted angrily, getting up to block my path, "I told you to leave-"

"Lily!" shouted a voice from down the hall.

My knees nearly buckled at the familiar, velvety sound. I stayed behind the guard as the crisp staccato of Mr. Brig's shoes approached with intense purpose. I could *feel* the comfort of his warm presence drawing near, just out of reach beyond the security guard.

"I apologize, Mr. Brig, I tried to stop her-"

Harrison swept past him and hugged me tightly. I buried my face into his torso. I could feel his abs pressing up against my cheek through his soft shirt.

"You should have called me, Simon," Harrison ordered firmly.

"I – yes, of course – I was just trying to protect you from-"

"I don't need protection from her, Simon. Now, if you want to protect your job, you'll apologize to-" He hesitated for half a second. "To my girlfriend."

I peeked one eye around Mr. Brig's chest to discover that the guard had turned a pale shade of gray.

"I'm-" he swallowed. "I'm so sorry, Miss," he responded very quietly. "Please let me know if there's anything I can do to make up for my lapse in judgment."

Harrison looked down at me. "Is there anything that this man can get you, Lily?" he asked loudly.

I swallowed. "Um. Hot chocolate usually calms me down," I explained in a voice barely loud enough to hear.

Mr. Brig looked up at the security guard. "Okay then. You can bring it up to my office.

With that, he whisked me down the hall.

I could feel the man staring at my back.

It was the first time seeing the inside of my boyfriend's office, and I would have been wowed by its presence in most circumstances. The mahogany desk at the head was polished to perfection, an elegant-looking bottle of whisky sat next to a crystal glass, his vast library was spread across the inlaid wood on every square inch of the walls, and his balcony had views that reached from the mountains to the foamy waves lapping the beach.

But I had eyes only for him.

I pounced the moment that his doorknob latched into place.

"Whoa, Lily!" he responded, grasping my wrists and holding me firm. I felt silly with my lips pursed in midair. "Why did you come?"

I relaxed my frame, slumping toward him. He did not let go of my arms.

I forced a wan smile. "I wanted to surprise my boyfriend at work, Mr. Brig."

He looked down at me sadly. "That's very nice of you, Lily, and I appreciate the gesture." He clenched his teeth. "It's just that I have a very busy day, and don't have a lot of time at the moment." He let me go, and I hung limply.

"Would you… like to wait on my couch and read a book?"

I didn't want to wait on his couch and read a book.

I waited on his couch and read a book.

It did not take long for me to get antsy and impatient.

I could feel him watching me out of the corner of his eye as I struggled with my dress, but he didn't understand what I was doing until I approached his desk.

He was on a phone call, so he couldn't react. His voice remained calm and professional as I opened his desk drawer, dropped my bra and panties into it, then walked back to the couch to continue reading.

And he continued talking.

So much of Mr. Brig remained a mystery, and that was one of the myriad reasons he would not leave my imagination. But a large part of him remained connected to me, and I swear that I could feel it in this moment. Strong, fleshy, vulnerable mental cords bound my mind to his, and I could taste the colorful tension that he felt.

I grabbed a piece of paper. I had never used a fountain pen before, but that's all he had ready, and I was willing to learn for him.

I wrote something down, pulled my hair into rubber bands, walked over to his desk, and dropped the note in front of him.

He didn't want to appear affected. And I'm nearly certain the person on the other end of the line couldn't tell any difference.

But eventually, his gaze wandered over to the note. His eyes took in every word, and I *felt* him squirm from fifteen feet away.

Mr. Brig – I just wanted you to know that I put my hair in pigtails because I want you to imagine grabbing them while I'm lying face-down on your desk with you inside of me.

Don't let that distract from your important phone call! ☺

-L

He did not look happy. That thrilled and terrified me. I was filled with perpetual doubt that I could affect him by even a fraction of the magnitude that I felt reciprocated from him, so I loved seeing any aspect of his life made different because of my influence. It was, in a way, very close to the joy I received from him spanking me: the bruises that he left were a tangible effect of the way that he had altered my life, and they were with me even when he was not.

But that self-doubt remained mercilessly omnipresent in my mind, perpetually telling me that I was not smart enough, not old enough, not *good* enough for the best man I had ever known. It told me that every response I forced from him was yet another step toward inevitable abandonment, and that in the very end I would have no one but myself to blame.

These intertwined emotional serpents tangled themselves around my mind, my heart, and my pussy in a relentless chokehold of feelings that I could only express as brattiness.

So when he refused to hang up the phone and pay attention to me, I would not accept it.

Instead, I walked over to his chair and sat on his lap. He tried to ignore me. A resultant hot, red flush rose to the surface of my skin, and my body moved three steps ahead of my brain.

I grinded my ass into his crotch, hoping to mimic the alluring way that strippers perform their trade in movies.

It wasn't that hard, because he was. I found my target with relative ease. I lifted my feet from the ground so that all of my body weight would concentrate on pushing his head between my asscheeks.

He released a soft gasp into the phone receiver.

Irritated, he lifted me from his lap and stood me in front of him.

I pouted. How was this fair? He regularly instructed me to serve whatever fleeting carnal desire overcame him in any given moment. Of this, there was no doubt.

I had recalled those vivid details several times while (I assumed) Emma was asleep and my idle finger found its way between my lower lips.

But now Mr. Brig turned away from me. I felt stupid.

So I tried again.

I sat on his desk, my feet dangling over the edge, and hiked the hem of my sundress up.

Way up.

Then I grabbed one of his fountain pens.

It wasn't as gratifying as Mr. Brig's touch, but it was just the right size to lie across my slit. I played my own pussy like a delicate violin, legs spread wide for his observation. I felt a wonderful thrill in knowing that I was violating his property.

Excitement overtook me as I drew my arm back farther – right into his bottle of whisky. It tumbled over, spilling across his desk. "Oh – I'm sorry, Mr. Brig, I'll clean it-"

He put the phone on mute, completely exasperated. "Lily! That was a Bruichladdich Octomore!"

My face flushed. "I'll finish cleaning it and buy you a new one-"

He looked sad, which was *so* much worse than angry. "No, *you* won't be able to, Lily." He sighed. "That was supposed to be my celebratory drink after this call. Please, just – let me finish here." He turned the phone off of mute.

I felt childish.

I wanted to cry, but I knew that would just prove my feelings correct. I needed to change my approach, and fast.

I needed to be more *adult,* so long as he was ready to handle it.

I rested my foot on his crotch. Even through the Vans, I had a very firm answer:

I was *affecting* him.

The sting of rejection battled with the thrill of forcing myself over his resistance, and my inner brat easily won the battle.

It's time, Inner Brat whispered into my ear, *to take what he's not willing to give.*

I didn't bother to pull the hem of my dress back down, opting instead to leave my bare ass exposed. I leaned over and spoke softly into his ear. "Don't fight me, Mr. Brig, unless you want the man on the phone to hear."

I could feel him tense up, and I liked it.

Then I crawled into the cavity below his desk and in front of his chair.

I had his belt unbuckled before he understood what was happening.

Mr. Brig tried to push me away as I unbuttoned his pants and lowered his zipper. I have no doubt that he would have tossed me aside like his little toy in other circumstances. But he had to maintain professionalism on the phone, and I was *very* determined, so he lost this particular struggle.

I folded his hands into mine, interlocking our fingers with a tight squeeze. I was anticipating a struggle to get his generous cock out of the pants with just one hand, but was happily surprised to find it nearly bursting for release. A long, thin, gossamer thread of precum told me that he had been resisting me with one head and longing for me with the other.

Even after weeks of dating, the size still intimidated me.

But I was so thirsty. I wanted to be impaled, to have my throat flirt with pain from the intensity, to *feel* him from the inside so deeply that the throbbing echoes of shared flesh would imprint themselves permanently on my mind and body alike.

I grabbed his dick with both hands, one on top of the other, barely able to wrap my fists around his unyielding girth. This cut in half the amount of cock waiting for my mouth, but it was still an intimidating prospect.

Mr. Brig gasped audibly into the phone as I slid my lips around him.

I could hear just enough of the conversation's other half to notice a sudden pause, followed by a question.

"Um," Mr. Brig gasped, "yes, I agree. It's just that I really, *really* like your suggestions for this project."

I bobbed faster, flitting the tip with my tongue, wanting and *needing* to consume every drop of the precum that I was responsible for creating. I never tired of knowing that part of my boyfriend had entered my body, that I had consumed it and become one with it.

Drool spilled uncontrollably from my gaping jaw. It slowly trickled down his shaft, dripping between my fingers in a growing torrent. I welcomed the intrusion as lubricant, and kneaded it between my fingers and I clenched and released my control over his most vulnerable part.

The fountain of slick, salty coating on the tip of his tongue seemed never-ending.

I bobbed faster.

"Well, Jameson, I think that we have a great plan on the table. Have your folks send the numbers over here, and we'll talk on Monday."

He hung up the phone without waiting for a goodbye.

Then Mr. Brig dropped his cell to the floor, stood up, and yanked me into a standing position. He moved so quickly that I don't think he realized that I hit my head against the desk on the way up.

I stood facing him, my dress still crumpled around my navel, his dick spanning the distance between us and grazing my torso just below my breasts. I looked up at him in momentary fear; his face was the picture of anger.

Then he spun me around and spanked my bare ass so hard that I saw stars. Before I knew what was happening, he had lifted me off the ground and laid me onto his desk in the prone position.

"Mr. Brig, I – *omph!*" I suddenly lost the power to speak as he slammed his dick into my vagina from behind.

Our previous experiences had been defined by a delicate gentleness, at least in the beginning, because my pussy was sensitive and inexperienced. There was none of that in this moment; I could feel his fiery passion pumping into me. It was frenzied, hurried, and angry.

Fortunately, I had been dripping wet for quite some time.

But the level of intensity was far greater than I had ever considered possible. He was finally, *finally* communicating the frustration that his words could not. He shared anger, irritation, hurt, and vulnerability by splitting me open in a raw and animalistic way that I did not know how to handle. I grasped the edges of the desk to stabilize myself in hopes of catching my breath. But Mr. Brig was having none of it; he grabbed my arms and pinned them behind my back, easily wrapping one hand around both of my tiny wrists.

I could not take in enough air to soothe my screaming lungs.

I could not draw enough breath to speak a single word.

I was terrified, imprisoned, and free.

He was *consuming* my body with the same ravenous hunger that led me to drink down every drop of his cum that I could taste. I adored feeling what he left behind deep inside my pussy, sloshing around the most intimate part of me even as we walked in public with passersby none the wiser.

And now he was responding in kind.

I wanted to tell him to own me, that every part of my body belonged to him, but to be gentle because I was afraid of just how much of me he'd taken already.

Suddenly, he pulled out. The sensation left me reeling.

Before I understood what was happening, he had pulled me off the table and stuffed me back under his desk. Papers fell to the floor, and the bottle of whisky teetered on the brink of falling over. I slumped against the side of the desk, as thoroughly spent as a book of used matches. I hazily watched as he stuffed his still-rigid cock back into his pants and struggled to zip it shut. It seemed an impossible feat, given the size of his erection, and he settled for covering himself with the bottom of his shirt.

I became aware of the growing staccato of an approaching pair high heels. Pushing me deep into the corner, Mr. Brig pulled his chair under the desk.

He was breathing hard.

The door creaked open. He tried, and failed, to steady his respiration.

A sultry, feminine voice met my ears, but she was standing on the other side of the desk, so we could not see each other. "Mr. Brig, I just talked with Mr. Jameson. He says that his phone call ended in a rather unorthodox-" She paused. "Is everything okay, Mr. Brig?"

He stumbled for words. "Yes, Angela, everything's-" He attempted to stand, but there was no discreet place to hide his prominent dick, so he immediately sat back down again. "Everything's quite wonderful, really. How – how are things with you?" He was still panting.

"I'm fine, we'll settle things with Mr. Jameson, it's just that – sir, are you certain that things are fine with your desk?" I heard her take an audible step closer.

"Yes, yes yes yes, everything's great. It's just that I – well, my pants zipper broke this morning, and I thought it was fixed, and – whoops! – it wasn't, so I'm, um, kind of dealing with that." His foot was tapping rapidly. It was just enough to vibrate the desk.

Which was just enough to send the whisky tumbling to the ground.

Angela reached out and deftly grabbed it in midair, crouching and stepping behind the desk to do so.

Bringing the two of us right into one another's line of sight.

My knees were pressed up against my face as though I could hide myself. I smiled with a weak mixture of guilt and shame.

She was intimidating as hell. Her whitish blonde hair was pulled back into a tight bun, accentuating the stark features of her businesslike expression. She looked to be in her late thirties, but exuded the intense authority of a woman twenty years older.

Slowly, she stood up and placed the bottle on the table. She and Mr. Brig shared a long, silent stare. It was apparent that they were sharing a completely silent conversation with nothing more than eye contact, and I felt a pang of jealousy land on top of my overwhelming embarrassment.

Angela finally broke the agonizing silence. "I'll just call Mr. Jameson back and explain that you were… temporarily under the weather, and will be back to normal soon."

Mr. Brig cleared his throat. "Yes, Angela, that will for the best."

She cast a glace down at me once more, then turned and walked briskly out the door. The sound of her crisp heels echoed down the hall.

Mr. Brig slid his chair back and reached out his hand. I took it and stood. Then he turned around, gently removed my bra and panties from his drawer, and handled them delicately to me. "I think you should leave, Lily," he explained with a softness that crushed me more than the loudest yelling ever could.

I felt ridiculous with my underwear in my hands. I didn't know whether to continue holding them, to put them on, or to throw them in the trash and run out the door screaming.

I reached out for a hug.

He gave me a half a hug with a quarter of his heart, and the whole of me was devastated.

"Mr. Brig, this – this didn't go how I'd planned, I – I just wanted to make a… a grand gesture," I finished lamely.

He looked ready to cry. "That's the problem, Lily," he sighed, and I could hear that he was more crushed than I was. "We'll talk on the phone tonight. For now, I have a business to run."

My eyes were growing heavy and hot. I knew that I had to stop the tears.

I couldn't stop the tears.

"No, Mr. Brig, *please* don't tell me you're giving up on me, on us, *please* don't tell me that."

He turned away, and I could have sworn that he wiped his eye. "We'll talk tonight, Lily."

I sobbed quietly. I needed an embrace that he wouldn't give.

We stood there, not looking at each other, not looking at anything, foolishly expecting to find easy answers to the question of how we chose to hurt each other.

"Why?" I asked in a quiet, gravelly voice. "Why wait until tonight?"

He struggled. "Sometimes it seems like things are clear. Hell, sometimes it seems like our own interpretation of what we *want* is clear. One of the greatest strengths we can develop is recognizing weakness in ourselves."

He turned and looked at me with sad eyes, weak eyes, proving that he *was* vulnerable to me, no matter how much he tried to deny it, and I understood that he was hiding it from me because he needed to hide it from himself.

It was a wonderfully terrible thing, and the most this moment could endure.

He took a step toward me, arms outstretched for a hug.

I turned from him and ran out the door.

Chapter Three

"And that's when *I* left," I sighed, feeling the tension coil and uncoil itself in my chest.

Carmen wiped away another of my tears, but did not otherwise interrupt me. I looked up at her face hovering above my own, then re-adjusted my head in her lap. "I knew from the beginning that he'd probably never agree to a date in the first place. I knew that even if the one-in-a-million shot of him *accepting* the date came up in my favor, it would never lead to…"

I could feel my face flushing, and Carmen's coy grin told me that my emotions lay bare in front of her. She rolled her thumb softly over my knuckles and squeezed my hand tighter, silently encouraging me to go on.

"So," I continued, exhausted but relieved to be sharing, "ever since we've been together, I've felt a *tension*. It's both bad and good – I don't know how to explain it. The stress pulled us toward each other, made the – um, you know – our *intimate* moments more electric, because we never knew what tomorrow would bring."

She wiped my eyes again.

"A drowning person will hug their life preserver with an intensity they never knew was possible. It was like that with us." I blinked several times, fighting back tears.

Carmen released my hand, wrapped hers softly around my arm, and interlocked our fingers from the other side. "But if you're right on the edge of drowning for weeks, eventually…" I drew in a deep, shuddering breath. "Well, that's the bad part."

I looked up, staring deeply into her brown eyes. "I wasn't afraid to be with him, because I had *no idea* that I could fall harder than I already had. But, Carmen…" She squeezed tighter. "I didn't realize how deep this could go."

She leaned back, gently rocking me in silence for a few minutes.

She broke it.

"Okay. Time to get up and fix things."

I stared up at her in surprise. "What? Did – did I tell the story wrong?"

She smiled. "Au contraire. You told it perfectly." She lifted my shoulders, bringing me into a sitting position. "Now you're going to get off this bed, put your shoes on, then walk outside and make it right."

I sat fully up and got off the bed, following her obediently but with great confusion. "Carmen, I don't think you – I don't think *I* understand what's going on."

She grabbed my hands, turning me toward her, holding my fingers gently but firmly. "You told me that he's always dated someone new and different, because no one could settle him down. No one could tame him. But there's always been the next woman who wanted to try. Am I right?"

A lone tear fell down my cheek. "That's always been his way."

"Before you."

I sniffed. "But we were only together a couple of months-"

"And he really, *really* didn't want to give you a chance to get into his head."

I shrugged.

"Or his pants."

I tried to cover my face with my hands, but Carmen grabbed them and held them firm.

"So the one girl whom he tried to run away from *actually caught him*. Do you see what I'm saying?"

"But you're not listening," I squirmed, "I *didn't* catch him. He's probably out with someone else now, she's probably a model who's a million times more beautiful than me." The tears flowed faster, and I was helpless to control them.

She dropped one hand and lifted my chin to focus her stare at me. "Lily, you cut that out right now. You *know* how people look at you." She took a long, deep breath. "You know that you're *desired*, that you're beautiful, and that most kids at this college would line up at the chance to chase after you."

A small sob escaped my lips. "I don't want most kids at this college. I want Harrison." I shook my head. "But he can do so much better than me. I feel so young and stupid for trying."

She dropped her grip on my chin and grabbed my shoulder. "Well if you try *again*, what you just said will only be half right." She let go of me, turned around, then marched to her dorm room door and opened it. "Now. Head out and make it happen."

I looked at her skeptically.

She rolled her eyes. "Are you really not *getting* it? *You* have something that's unique to who *you* are, Lily. It was enough to make him stop dating other women, even if it was for a short time. It was enough for him to overcome his inhibitions when he thought that you were taboo. And it's enough for you to fix this problem if you really love him as much as you claim." She raised an eyebrow. "But the door won't stay open for long."

I breathed deeply, tears still flowing.

Then I closed my eyes and nodded. I could feel my ponytail, now greatly disheveled from Carmen's lap, bobbing wildly behind me.

"Okay," I breathed. "Okay. Tomorrow's Saturday, so he'll be home. I've tried a one-in-a-million chance before." I wiped my eyes. "But I'll need your help if I'm going to do something ridiculous again."

She smiled.

I bit my lip nervously, squinting in the noonday sun. I wondered if I should have dressed differently; I could *feel* him staring at me whenever I wore a black dress and heels.

I looked down again at my t-shirt, shorts, and Converse.

No, this was the right choice.

This was me.

That fact caused another wave of doubts, which I alleviated by staring at my phone.

Nothing can compare to the nerves that result from waiting on a text from someone who has thrown you completely head over heels. It's basically a tense conversation stretched from five minutes into three hours.

I wondered how Harrison could possibly have handled dating before text flirting existed. I was struck with vertigo when I thought of the years he'd experienced in ways that I would never understand, encompassing a time greater than twice my entire life, filled with stories that I could never hope to know in their entirety.

My phone buzzed. A shot of adrenaline shot through my chest with such intensity that it physically hurt. I struggled to keep my hand steady enough to read the texts.

<Hey. ☺ I'm outside ur place right now. Can u come out to talk?>

<Hello, Lily. I wasn't aware of the fact that you were planning to drop by. I'll come down to let you in.>

This was it. It hurt to hope, and it hurt *not* to hope. The combination of fiery adrenaline and cold dread mixed in my torso to create a lukewarm concoction of human misery.

A couple of years prior, we had studied American Literature as part of our junior year requirement. One of the assignments had come from a Puritan writer who talked about sinners dangling from divine fingertips, clinging to hope with their entire being.

And still, despite the fear, the vulnerable ones expressed complete love and devotion. My classmates had agreed that the people in the story were stupid to accept control from such a whimsical fate, but I thought there was no better way to describe love.

The door opened, and I was weak.

Lust causes us to gawk at every beautiful detail in a beautiful person, drinking up the finer points of their honed edges as they impress their idealized physique on a hungry mind like the sizzling burn of a red-hot branding iron. Those rose-tinted memories wander into our thoughts in the most passionate moments, filling any contours that our craving minds imagine to be empty.

Love is entirely the same, yet wholly different. Loving someone means sacrificing a part of yourself, cutting deeply and mercilessly to hand over a piece that may or may not be rejected by a person whose influence might as well be divine. That person will trigger lust in all circumstances; instead of waiting for passionate moments, it will *create* them, rendering the person plagued with love entirely vulnerable, controlled, and very, very thirsty.

So when Harrison emerged from the door wearing a sweater and jeans, I swooned at the way they fell perfectly on his body. I asked myself, distantly, why his appearance was so perfect in this moment. The answer antagonized me, but I knew that it was entirely accurate:

Because.

I steadied my knees as he walked toward me, purposeful yet sad, and I wondered if I was ready to face him. I'd wondered the same thing the first time he spread my legs apart, realizing that he was about to split me open in a way that I wasn't sure I could handle. He had seemed far too big for me in that moment, and I was sure that I would break trying to take him in.

I had been right.

He reached out and clutched my elbow. I wrapped my other arm around his waist, grabbing him low enough and close enough to be intimate without allowing vulnerability.

He struggled to find words. I waited until he was about to speak, then cut him off at the last moment.

"I've been trying to understand what makes me different from other women," I began, voice shaking, "and it's hard. Most girls grow up with an implied understanding that some part of us will never be good enough, that we're secretly ugly somehow, and that it's our job to hide that fact from the world." I breathed in and out slowly as he listened patiently. "So instead, I tried to articulate what makes *you* different, but my thoughts got so jumbled that I wanted to *act* instead of speak, resulting in me hiding under your desk during that phone call. So I was again at a loss." My voice steadied, and I smiled. "Then I changed my mind, and asked what makes *us* different, Harrison. Is there some magic element that spares us pain?" My smile stayed in place, but felt sadder. "No – there isn't. We're subject to the same reality that pulls couples apart every day, no matter how invincible they once felt." I squeezed his back, then dropped my arm and stepped aside. "But what I want from you – and for us – *is* what's real, not something that can be idealized in a moment. There is no single magic bullet, and neither one of us can succeed in a relationship on behalf of us both." My hands were shaking, so I hid them behind my back. He glanced, very briefly, at my chest; for half a second, I felt powerful. "All we can have – all *anyone* can have – is a multitude of small things that make life better in a way that would otherwise go unfulfilled."

He hid his mouth behind his hand, and I like to think that he was smiling despite his best efforts.

"So," I continued, growing bolder, "I can't do any one thing to make up for ruining your afternoon yesterday." I could feel my face growing red, but I plowed ahead anyway. "But I thought you'd enjoy a small thing that made *today* a little better."

I cast my eyes down, clasped my hands together, then rotated my entire body as a way of sheepishly pointing. Mr. Brig slowly turned to look in the same direction.

A short distance away from us, a man leaned against a very shiny silver car. He was old, probably in his forties, and clearly put as much effort into his wardrobe as Harrison did. Arms folded, eyebrow raised, he looked caught between curiosity and amusement.

It was not often that Harrison expressed genuine shock, so I relished the fleeting moments when they came.

Particularly when I was the cause.

"Is that – is he here to meet me?"

I smiled shyly. "Why don't you go ask him?"

We walked side-by-side without holding hands.

"Harrison Brig," the man said, extending his arm. "I heard that you work seven days a week over at the Brig Corporation. Why on earth are you taking a Saturday morning off?"

Harrison shook the man's hand confidently. "Nolan Radner, I presume. Why the hell are you *not* driving that Jaguar XJ220 on a Saturday morning?"

Nolan leaned his head in my direction. "Lily here was very insistent that I should meet you for a chat about my collection."

Harrison stared at me so hard that his eyes look ready to pop. "You know *Nolan Radner*?"

I didn't realize how excited I had gotten until I heard my own voice. "Yes. I mean, no. Yes, I asked him to come and meet you, but I didn't know him before, he just agreed when I told him that no one would appreciate him like you could."

Shit. That sounded wrong. "I mean, I knew that if I talked to him-"

"She was waiting by my car," Nolan jumped in. "I assumed that she wasn't running a scheme to steal the XJ220, but maybe she's a *really* good con artist." He winked at me.

Harrison was flabbergasted. "But – how did you know where his car was, and when he'd be there?"

I stared at my feet. "Um. Well, you told me which car was his, and it's easy to notice when it's parked nearby, so I waited for him to come back to it."

Harrison's voice was growing with concern. "And how *long* did you wait by his car?"

I shook my head. "That's – really not important. Anyway, he was skeptical at first, but it turns out he likes the other thing I brought for you, and maybe you two could share it."

I don't know how to describe the look on Harrison's face, but I had never seen it before.

Nolan reached through the open window and produced a bottle.

Harrison laughed, and the slight sound nearly tore me apart. The idea that he might be laughing *at* me made me want to run and hide, but the thought of him laughing *with* me stopped my breath. "Is that a bottle of-"

"Bruichladdich Octomore, yes. It took me ten minutes to learn how to say it, and one of Carmen's 21-year-old friends had to buy it at the store, but I found it."

He took the whisky from Nolan, then looked down at me in concern. "This is an expensive Scotch."

I glanced back up and smiled. "Doesn't matter. Some things cost much more to lose."

A brief moment of silence hung over us.

"Well," Nolan interjected, "based on what Lily has told me, you've got a lot of insight about my collection. Most people who come through my garage are either faking knowledge or trying to get money out of me, so to be honest, it would be a nice to show it to someone without worrying about an ulterior motive."

"Does trying to drink my whisky count as an ulterior motive?" Harrison joked in response.

Nolan genuinely laughed. "Lily has great taste," he explained.

I waited for Harrison to reveal that it was a lie, that I didn't understand anything about a world that was too big to notice me, and that I had acted incredibly childish by putting this all together.

"Yes," came his response. "She has exquisite taste."

My heart soared so high that I couldn't feel my legs.

"Nolan, can I have a moment with Lily?"

Harrison walked a few feet away with me by his side. I knew that the safe thing would be to let him speak.

But sometimes, the safe thing will get you killed.

"I can't promise that I'll always say or do the right thing, Harrison," I began. "I'm younger than you would like a girlfriend to be." I took his hands in mine and looked up into his eyes. "But that means I'm at a point where I'm willing to learn. And *believe* me, I learned a *lot* yesterday about what not to do, and how not to do it. I'm not set in my ways, but that doesn't mean I'm lost."

He said nothing, but I could see the internal brawl raging behind his eyes. A lifetime of practicality battled with raw lust, and I believed that the resilient bud of blossoming love lurked just behind as an arbiter of the storm.

I rested my hand on his cheek. "What I can give you, Harrison – what I can give *us* – is not just a willingness, but a *need* to listen to the most important parts of the story that make you who you are. I promise to hear what's important when the rest of the world is too afraid of being close enough to get hurt. I *know* that you can hurt me, but I care more about sparing *you* pain. If you can find a woman who says that with more confidence than me, you take her, Harrison Brig, and you never look back."

I didn't notice him closing the distance between us; all I knew is that we were kissing, and it was nothing like a passionate embrace at the end of a Hollywood story. It was raw and earthly, composed of a violent clash of the masculine and feminine, the inevitable effect of two people finally failing to resist the call of the missing piece that each had left inside the other.

He was angry at me for the way I made him feel, and angry at himself for succumbing to that feeling.

I pulled away, gasping for air, and stared at him with the visceral intent of a hunter about to claim the prey in her trap. "Later," I breathed. "Go play with your new friend."

I gave the slightest tug on his dick before turning around, smiling to myself once he couldn't see me.

I *love* forcing him into awkward public situations with an unfulfilled rail spike in his pants.

"Well, Harrison," came Nolan's voice from behind me as I headed out of sight, "it must be hard to see a woman like that walking away from you."

It was my first time eating with Emma since she'd walked in on me naked and riding my boyfriend's face, but I really wanted to attempt feeling normal with my roommate again. She sat across from me in the college dining hall at De Neve Plaza; Carmen sat on my left, and several of our friends had joined us. One of them, a sophomore named Jordan, had been trying unsuccessfully to flirt with Carmen for the past three weeks. He would have benefitted from more rigorous grooming standards, but that is a skill set most college boys lack.

"I never understood why professors sometimes use the dining halls," Jordan explained confusedly. "Do they think it makes them look cool?" He grunted.

"Doubtful, it's having no effect on you," Carmen muttered under her breath.

Emma snorted into her creamed potatoes while Jordan stared uncomprehendingly at Carmen.

Then Emma froze, wide-eyed, at something over my shoulder. "That's… not a professor."

Not understanding, I turned around to see what had caught her attention.

Then I, too, froze.

Harrison was wandering among the tables, clearly searching for me. What the fuck was he doing here?

He caught my eye, smiled, and approached.

"What's wrong with your face, Lily?" Jordan asked. "It just got *extremely* red."

Carmen reached under the table and squeezed my hand, calming me slightly.

Emma finally spoke up. "That's Lily's-"

"Hi!" Harrison explained to the group. "I'm Lily's boyfriend." He looked around at the crowded table. "My, there aren't seats anywhere. Could I squeeze in?"

Carmen looked up at Harrison, eyebrows raised, then glanced back at me approvingly. "You can take my seat, Mr. Brig, I was just going to get up and grab another drink." She slowly stared him up and down. "I suddenly got very thirsty."

She stalked away, and he squeezed in next to us. "Glad to meet you folks," he offered brightly, scanning the table. "You and I never officially met. I'm Harrison," he explained to Emma, offering his hand. "I was indisposed when we crossed paths earlier."

She shook it graciously.

I had always dreamed of showing off my boyfriend, but this was...

Awkward.

Then I felt his hand on my inner thigh, and things got *more* awkward very quickly. Was he really going to slide his fingertips along my soft flesh, igniting the overlooked nerves that trace a path from my knees to my panties, by moving at a pace just slow enough and just gentle enough to distract my thoughts?

I snapped my focus back to the table.

Everyone was staring at me.

And Mr. Brig was still dancing his hand along my leg. The shorts I was wearing offered no resistance has he freely roamed. I had no idea if anyone could see it.

That sent a flutter through my stomach. I hated the feeling, because I felt self-conscious and embarrassed – but I loved it too. I loved the control that I hated to sacrifice, and my head was muddled by the fact that lust for him scrambled my ability to think clearly while he exercised control over me in a public place. Why would he do this to me?

Oh.

I reached under the table and clutched his hand in mine. He grabbed me tightly, interlocking our fingers and rolling his thumb softly over my knuckle.

"Well, Harrison," Emma asked, looking both flustered and amused, "where did you and Lily meet?"

"Yoga class," he immediately responded with a smile. "I've always had a hard time stretching beyond my comfort zone, but she taught me that limits can be pushed much further than I once believed." He grabbed a carrot off my plate and took a bite. "But even if it seems hard at first, perhaps occasionally too much to endure, it's worth the benefit in the end."

He slipped his fingers free of my grasp, then slid them dangerously close to my crotch. I grabbed his hand with both of mine, and I could feel his skin breaking as I dug my nails into him.

He paused, breathing in slowly.

He *liked* it.

I was momentarily shocked by his enjoyment, but then I remembered the first bruises he'd left on my bare ass. I'd ogled them in the mirror for a week after Mr. Brig had spanked me, and mourned their passing as they slowly faded into obscurity. I imagined digging my nails deeply into his chest, cutting him, *marking* him as he leaned over me with a little black whip and turned my ass from a blank canvass into his blue and purple work of art.

"Is that right, Lily?"

Damn it. He'd intruded so deeply into my thoughts that I was unable to focus on the world around me. I hated how much he knew that I was his plaything in this moment.

"Um. Yep," I responded with faked confidence.

"Oh, that's great! There are at least a dozen of us who would *love* to have you teach us yoga," Emma answered happily.

I smiled blankly. "Ah. That sounds like it would be much fun."

Harrison gave one last squeeze of my thigh, then brought his hand to the table. It was *very* clearly marked and bleeding from where I'd cut him. I was embarrassed, proud, and thrilled.

"Well," Harrison added cheerfully, "I've eaten my fill, and I must be going." He turned, kissed my lips with an abbreviated passion, then got up to leave.

"Wait," Jordan said as he walked away while I hid my face in my hands, "I don't get it. Is he a professor of yoga?"

It's both agonizing and wonderful to be so overtaken by another person that your mind cannot escape their grasp, even while alone. Those moments are even worse, in a certain way, than being overwhelmed by their presence. In the absence of what's real, our minds create the most perfectly tantalizing interactions with a person so intoxicating that we often doubt whether they actually exist outside of our own imaginations.

Before we'd started dating, I'd slipped my panties into his pocket while he was out with another woman. Had he felt the way I did right now? Did he hate the way he loved me?

I pulled apart every sentence, every word that had passed between us in the dining hall.

Where was the proof that he loved me as much as I loved him?

I was so deep inside my own thoughts that the buzzing text alert made me jump.

<Hello, Lily. I'm glad to be inside your head.>

What could I possibly say in response? That he was utterly, totally, entirely right? That my mind was completely at his mercy, craving absolutely any interaction that would make him feel closer, even for a moment?

Buzz

Hands shaking, I looked down at the phone again.

<I want you to be an obedient girl, Lily. Tell me that you will.>

My heart rate slowed with focused intent. The jitters flowed from my fingertips as I embraced the idea of allowing my body to be controlled.

<I will obey anything you order, Mr. Brig.>

The next two minutes were agonizing. I made my way back into my dorm room and lay down on my bed, mind racing at the question of what he might command.

Struck by a sudden memory, I lay my phone against my shorts over my crotch. I pressed down, pushing my pussy lips apart and squeezing my clit.

I waited.

BUZZ

The vibrations made it apparent just how wet my lips currently were. Now that I'd begun, I was in no way inclined to cease. I slid my left hand below my panties, slowly drawing my fingertip along the outer folds as I closed in on my clit.

Once I got there, I pressed and held.

Breathing came in short, choppy bursts as I pushed a stationary finger into myself, imagining the sensation of Mr. Brig's dick in the exact same place at the moment just before impaling me.

I turned my head to read his text.

<Touch yourself tonight. Bring yourself to the very edge of completion, but do NOT finish. Be teased. Don't spoil what's to come.>

I whined audibly, nearly screaming.

Then I regained control. I slowed my breathing.

I wanted to cum. Desperately.

But the excitement of being controlled on such an intimate level brought me beyond the physical thrill. Mr. Brig was inside of me mentally. It was far more raw than "making love." He was *fucking* me, and he was doing it without even being in the room.

I texted back.

<Yes, sir. Would you like photographic evidence as proof of my obedience?>

I slid under the covers, pulled my shorts and panties off, and tossed them to the floor. Now wearing nothing but a t-shirt and ankle socks, I rested the phone on my bare pussy.

I waited, obediently, for the next buzz.

Chapter Four

I didn't want Emma to hear me masturbating, so I buried my face in the pillow and bit down on the cloth.

Hard.

That would have been bearable in the right doses.

But Mr. Brig forced me to play with myself for three hours before I could stop. Emma was on the bunk above me, so I had to be extra quiet.

And I didn't think of disobeying.

Two days before, I had been *certain* Mr. Brig was ready to leave me forever. But knowing that he wanted to play this game proved he wasn't finished with me - at least not yet.

So I blindly followed his lead, riding the high of being controlled while knowing that I was teetering along the sheer edge of a precipice that could lead directly to the greatest disappointment of my life.

I danced along the threshold.

Each time that I was about to cum, he instructed me to text him. Inevitably, he ordered a five-minute "cooling off" period that only agonized me further. Each time that I felt it was impossible to continue without cumming on my fingers, he demanded obedience.

I gave him everything.

And in the end, after taking all of me, he sent one final text.

<You're a good girl. Do not touch yourself any more tonight. Wait patiently for next weekend.>

A solitary tear of pure frustration fell down my cheek.

Then I smiled, turned over, and fell into a night of agonizingly beautiful dreams.

I was sitting absentmindedly in my psychology class, ignoring whatever the T. A. was saying, when I finally understood the things I had been feeling.

Harrison had found a way to crawl inside my head and refuse to leave. No matter how agonizing his grasp was, my attempts to ignore the thought of him proved impossible. His presence in my social life was even more awkward, because he didn't fit.

But he pushed anyway.

And I knew that I would accept his intrusion, just as firmly as I knew that the sun would spring up tomorrow. There was no denying why this was the case.

I was weak.

It was mind-blowing to consider how one human being could be pure kryptonite to another. My draw toward him transcended the concept of desire. After all, I didn't breathe air just because I *wanted* it.

I thought about how he would behave if he were feeling the same thing.

My pussy tensed involuntarily.

<We will have dinner in my office. This Friday at 9:00. You may choose your own outfit for the evening; all other aspects will be at my discretion.>

I knew what he was doing. Allowing the slightest feeling of autonomy would wrap me around his finger tighter than complete submission would. The hungry person is most ravenous when food is close enough to *almost* taste it.

My single choice had to be the right one, so I checked the weather for that night.

It was going to be unseasonably hot.

I walked confidently past Simon the security guard as I approached Mr. Brig's office. Simon nodded slightly as I passed, but otherwise showed no reaction to my presence on his turf.

The building seemed to be otherwise empty as I approached the office door. I steadied my hand before knocking.

It opened a crack. "Thank you, Simon," Mr. Brig's voice reverberated from inside. "You may go home for the evening. I think I can handle this on my own."

From behind me, I heard the man get up and quickly leave.

I pushed against Harrison's door and stepped into the dimly lit room.

A lamp sat on a table in the far corner. Two plates with serving dish covers sat upon the table, waiting to be opened.

Mr. Brig closed the door behind me, leaning on one arm that he rested against the wooden frame.

I nearly gasped when I saw him, but managed not to show it.

His black suit melted into a black shirt that blended into a black tie. Every stich had clearly been woven to fit his frame, because it hugged the contours of his body, rippled across his abs, and wrapped itself around his waist tightly enough to make me jealous.

He looked down at me in hunger and judgment. "This is the outfit that you chose for tonight?" he asked skeptically.

I glanced over my own body. My dark overalls ended in shorts, contrasting with a very comfy white t-shirt. The white Vans were my favorite pair.

"No," I responded confidently, showing him my backpack. "My outfit for tonight's in here."

He nodded slowly. "My office has a bathroom right behind you. Hurry up and change; we want to eat while it's hot."

I moved quickly. The beauty in me that I saw reflected in his eyes was a standard that seemed impossible to meet, so I had to act before the worst of my doubts could overtake the best of his lust.

I left the backpack behind me as I emerged from the bathroom.

"Have a seat, Lily, it's time to eat," he called from across the room. "Now, let's see what you had in that backpack-" He stopped as I emerged into view.

"What did I have in there?" I echoed. "Nothing."

I walked confidently over to the table. The cold, wooden floor sent a chill through my bare feet that traveled up my sides and caused the slighted shiver in my shoulders. My nipples were hardening, but I didn't know if that was a reaction to temperature or vulnerability.

Mr. Brig froze, clearly taken aback. I instinctively tried to bury my smile behind a collar or sleeve, and felt even more naked upon reaching for something that wasn't there.

"Lily, what are you doing?" he asked in surprise. "I told you that-"

"I could choose my outfit for the evening," I responded innocently. "And I feel that this selection most authentically represents who I am."

He hid any reaction.

"Well," I asked with a smile, "let's sit down. I think we both have an appetite."

Mr. Brig had been confident that he would be directing every aspect of this date, and I relished watching him struggle for self-control.

I *did* want him to dominate the evening, to be sure.

But I wanted to watch him work for it.

We sat across from each other, and he told me to uncover my food. It proved to be a lovely wood-roasted chicken infused with white truffles and brioche. I inhaled deeply; it was, truly, culinary perfection on level that would forever ruin the thought of dining hall food. I looked up to watch my boyfriend's reaction.

He was staring at my tits.

I spread my arms wide under the guise of innocently stretching, making my chest as prominent as possible.

I was daring him to restrain himself.

I was daring him to react.

Instead, he cleared his throat and focused on his own meal.

I smiled, then picked up a spoonful of cranberry sauce. Suddenly, it slipped off and landed on my chest.

Fortunately, I wasn't wearing anything that would stain.

The piece of cranberry landed on my right breast and slid down to my nipple. It was delightfully icy cold, and I told myself that I would have to remember this sensation for the future. Then I lifted my finger to the stained nipple, wiped my breast with a strong, smooth stroke, leaving a faint, glistening residue in its wake. I closed my eyes, placed my finger in my mouth, and sucked the sweetness down.

The air suddenly became charged as though a lighting bolt was about to tear the room apart. I felt it weighing down on my body with a tension I did not immediately understand.

I opened my eyes to see Mr. Brig standing above me, his face contorted with a mixture of torment and deep hunger.

I immediately felt tiny and defenseless beneath him.

And very, very naked.

He reached down, grabbed my hand, and lifted me out of the chair. I stood, very aware of the fact that he could easily have taken me with minimal effort.

I had played a bold hand, and it came at a price:

I was now completely subject to whatever momentary whims passed Harrison's mind.

He lowered his head to my chest, and I gasped as he pulled my right nipple into his mouth. His tongue worked furiously, finding every trace of the sugary bitter residue and tracing its path up my breast.

I tried to control my breathing. I really did. But my nerves built upon each other like swelling ocean waves as his tongue pressed against my chest, neck, and cheek. He finally descended on my mouth, kissing me hungrily, and I nearly leapt up to embrace him.

But he grabbed my wrists and held me firm, pinning my arms against my sides. I wanted to tell him that he was being unfair, that there was no reason to restrict my arms while my lips were fulfilled, but my mouth was too occupied to speak.

Then he pulled back and lifted me with great ease. He shoved his own dinner plate aside. It crashed to the ground with a clatter, but he was far too focused on the meal at hand to care. Then Mr. Brig laid me down on the dinner table, resting one hand on my neck and sliding the other one toward my crotch. Instead of watching what was happening below, I focused on his face.

Whatever he did to my body would be based on his own discretion.

I felt his fingers wind their way down to my leg, then slowly approach my crotch. My breathing picked up as I felt him closing in.

I watched him as he worked with concentration and purpose. As he placed his hands on my pussy lips, I braced for his fingers' entrance.

Instead, he spread my lips open. I shuddered as the cool air met my slick, exposed inside, now on display for him.

"Your breathing is too loud, Lily. Be silent for me."

That was hard. I wanted to submit to every request, but my heart was beating way to quickly for me to maintain self-control. "I'm sorry, Mr. Brig. Would you like me to wear a gag for you?"

That was the spark.

He grabbed both of my hands and ripped me off the table, standing me upright. Then he turned me around, pinned my arms behind my back, and forced me to walk.

That didn't slow my breathing.

But I followed, obediently, until I realized where he was taking me.

"Mr. Brig, your balcony's *outside*-"

"And that's exactly where you're going," he responded authoritatively.

I didn't think I was ready for it.

But then he opened the doors, and suddenly I realized that I was *quite* capable. The warm night air caressed my nude body, kissing my nipples before sliding around my waist and gently cupping my lower cheeks.

He closed the door behind us and continued to push me forward.

And he brought us right to the edge.

We stopped next to the wall that protected people from falling twenty stories down. From this view at the top floor, the effect was dizzying; cars crawled below us like tiny cogs in a greater machine.

My breasts were higher than the short wall, and it appeared very likely that I could be viewed from other buildings if anyone knew where to look. It seemed crazy *not* to run back inside.

But I remained where I was.

Mr. Brig slowly raked his fingernails up my arms, leaving a wave of goosebumps in their path. He reached down to kiss my neck, and the gentle effect of the two sensations was sublime. The physical stimulation intertwined with the knowledge that someone *might* be watching and induced an intoxicating brew of excitement and vulnerability that put me on the brink of finishing what had been building for an entire week.

Face still nestled in my neck, Mr. Brig drew my arms forward a placed them on the wall in front of me. The connection between my skin and the outside world forced an unrelenting sensation of nudity; the cold stone touching my palms and smooth cement beneath my soles emphasized that nothing was covering me. The world could see me as I was, regardless of whether that was vulgar, beautiful, or both.

I stood, leaning forward, and wondered what Mr. Brig would do to me next.

It turns out that he wanted to skip the foreplay.

I whimpered as I felt his dick slide inside of me, realizing with shock as his thighs hit my ass that *he filled me with his entire gigantic cock on the first thrust.* I had certainly *felt* wet on a nonstop basis all week, and he seemed delighted to find no resistance as he entered me completely.

His lips were directly next to my ear as he released a supremely satisfied groan. The deep reverberations sent a chill down my spine that was amplified with the knowledge that *I* was responsible for the sound.

I vaguely realized that we were both moaning, my high pitch harmonizing with his low one. But the reality is that I couldn't notice my own noise independently; it felt like *we* were making the sounds, and that it was impossible to separate my actions from his.

I worked with him as he built momentum with each thrust into my vagina. It was intense, even painful, for me, but I could *feel* the pleasure radiating down his cock. That physical satisfaction was more than enough to mask my own pain, and I absorbed his thrusting joyfully.

"More, Mr. Brig," I moaned. "Tear me apart."

The encouragement spurred him on. He grabbed my arms and pulled them wide before forcing me to step to the edge. He pressed my stomach against the wall, my tits grazing the stony edge from above as I tilted forward and looked at the ground below.

My head spun with vertigo and fear as I leaned forward, but he held my arms secure. I knew that I was safe with *almost* no doubt, but the feeling of danger spiked my heart rate higher than I thought it could go.

He pounded faster.

His suit brushed up against my bare back, yet again eliciting a feeling of nakedness in front of someone fully clothed. The exposure, submission, and danger built upon themselves. I was ready to release a week's worth of cum, screaming into the night without caring who saw or heard me.

Then he slid out, and I wanted to scream for a different reason altogether.

He pulled me by the wrist to a corner of the building. A tall, thin pole protruded from the wall at that point, and a built-in bench nestled up against the corner. Before I understood what was happening, Mr. Brig had made me stand on the bench, then followed me from behind. The edge of the wall was now at my knee level, and I instinctively grabbed the pole for support.

He whipped off his belt, slid it around me, and fastened me to the pole, ensuring that I would be secure if I slipped.

But that didn't prevent it from being *terrifying*.

My heart was now beating faster than what I had believed to be its limit. Looking down, all I could see was the ground far below, with the wall mostly invisible at knee level.

But I could feel him wrapped around me. I was afraid, but comforted. I leaned back into his soothing embrace. The knowledge that he had strapped me in, so now *he* was vulnerable to falling, drew me to him in a way that I would never have suspected possible.

Mr. Brig pulled me in tightly as we looked over the edge and he entered me once more.

This time, I could not work with his thrusting. All of my focus went into grasping the pole, holding myself as still as possible despite how hard I was being pounded.

Perhaps it was the fear, but Mr. Brig was relentless. With each hip gyration, he withdrew his penis nearly in its entirety, then slid back inside of me until his waist collided against my asscheeks. Each piston thrust seemed to take a fraction of a second, and I struggled to hold my body still as he railed against me.

The city was almost perfectly silent at this height; only my high-pitched gasping, his deep grunts of effort, and the violent slapping of flesh against flesh penetrated the night sky. My nerves were spent from a combination of the fear of looking down, the ravaging of my pussy, and the complete vulnerability of placing the sanctity of my body with a man who simultaneously revered it and *needed* to rip it open.

He had brought me to the edge. The sounds sent me over.

I screamed into the black night as I finally, *finally* came after a week of relentless teasing. The risk of falling suddenly seemed very real, but Mr. Brig grasped me powerfully in his arms and held me firm against the pole. In that tight embrace, he thrust desperately, as though he could only ensure our safety by penetrating me to even deeper levels.

Then he dropped one hand and found my clit.

All physical orientation flowed out of my body. The twin sensations of vaginal penetration and fingers on my clit overrode any understanding of where I was standing or which direction gravity was pulling. I leaned further into his chest, trusting the man I loved most to keep me from falling as I sailed over the peak.

That sensation of trust, combined with the feeling on my clit, brought the second orgasm. The first one hadn't really ended, so this second one took the flame and poured gasoline on it. I bounced back and forth between screaming and laughing, but I only knew this to be true as a result of *hearing* it, not because I felt the conscious decision of making those sounds. All physical control of my body had been handed over to Mr. Brig at this point. The line between his body and mine had been blurred when his most vulnerable parts became one with the inside of my torso, and I shuddered with lust to think about just how deep inside of my body he was at the moment. And by ceding control of safety, my mind had been overtaken and intermingled with his. Everything we were was bound together, and in that oneness, I felt that I had found my true self for the first time.

He slid out of me, wrapped himself even tighter, then unbuckled his belt. With a delicate strength, he carried me down from the bench and brought me into a sitting position. I expected the cold sensation of concrete to meet my ass, but was shocked to find soft blankets and a cushion ready to meet me. I looked at him questioningly. Eye contact was all we needed to communicate, though. I understood immediately that he had planned all week to ravage me outdoors, and had been yearning for this as much as I had, tinged with the desperation of being perpetually close to the edge for so long.

I understood that he, too, had decided not to cum all week.

And he hadn't yet finished tonight.

In this moment, no longer riding along the harsh edge, I realized that *I* could be the caretaker of a man who craved the soft caress of a blanket and the warm touch of femininity.

I pushed him gently back, and he only gave the softest resistance before relaxing onto the mattress.

I straddled his waist and lowered my pussy onto his dick once more, beaming as a wide, satiated grin broke across his face. I didn't thrust; instead, I held that position as I slowly leaned forward and unbuttoned his shirt. I took my time as I worked my way down, button by button. Without a doubt, I absolutely loved the thrusting. But that did not discount the joy of its opposite. The intense sliding in and out was built on intensity; what I did now was based on comfort and intimacy. I took my time, enjoying each quiet second as it passed. Sitting, patiently unmoving, with his dick inside of me made it feel like it *belonged* there. The eroticism stemmed from the fact that it *wasn't* intense. In this moment, it was the most natural thing in the world for his dick to be resting deep inside me as I intimately took care of the man I loved.

Eventually, I got his jacket, tie, and shirt off his body. Then I leaned back to remove his shoes and socks, keeping his dick inside of me where it belonged, but exposing the penetration to his dazed expression as I leaned far back.

With that accomplished, I slid off of him, immediately missing his warmth like I was rolling out of a frothy hot tub and into the chilly night with no towel. I quickly slid his underwear over his massive erection, nearly ripping the waistband with the strain, then pulled the underwear and pants over his ankles and threw them aside.

I immediately impaled myself back onto his dick, and we both groaned at the exact same frequency. The grin on his face told me that my own smile was just glowing just as bright.

I clutched his cheeks with both hands, lowered my face, and kissed him. It wasn't the raw, animalistic assault that he had given me outside his apartment; this kiss spoke of calm intimacy and belonging. There was no urgency in the particular moment; we were together when the fire burned hottest, and now we were watching the glowing embers as they embraced us in their cozy warmth.

I pulled back from the kiss and laid my head on his chest. I wanted to stay like that forever; his dick in my pussy felt like the missing piece of my body that I'd always needed, and I hated the fact that the bond would have to eventually be broken.

But I needed to take care of him. I'd trusted him at the edge, and he trusted me when we were grounded.

I sighed contentedly, then slid off of his dick.

I looked down to watch; I adored seeing his penis enter and exit me. Upon extracting myself, a gossamer strand of intermingled fluid stretched and drooped between his dick and my pussy. That lone point of connection possessed such vulgar beauty that I wanted to dive into his arms and beg him to keep up on the roof with him forever. We would be far away from an unyielding world that lacked the trust needed to cross an edge with nothing but your other half.

He ran his fingers through my hair, and I smiled. He was desperate for me, but now I was in control, and things would happen on my whims.

Mr. Brig had placed his faith in my control. He stared up at me hungrily, waiting to be eaten.

I pulled my pussy back, stretching the string of fluid far longer than I thought it would go, before it finally broke. I was already standing at this point, so I took two steps back, then kneeled down in front of him.

His dick was so coated in my juices that it shimmered in the moonlight.

'Well,' I thought as I descended on him, 'I *did* skip dinner.'

I started at the base of his dick, gently pulling it toward me as I drew my tongue all the way to his tip. He moaned as I drew the fluid into my mouth.

It didn't taste good because of the *flavor*. No, the delectable aspect of what coated my tongue was the knowledge of what it meant. The flavor was earthy, raw, salty, and human. His own unforgiving masculinity swirled with the unfamiliar yet intimate taste of my pussy.

I smiled and swallowed. Harrison whimpered.

I dove in for more.

Giving head to Mr. Brig had always been a hard task; but now that I had tried it several times, I was mostly excited and only slightly scared at the prospect. I had a relatively tiny jaw for my age, and his dick was as long as the distance between my teeth and the back of my head.

It was a challenge. But to be honest, I think he enjoyed watching me struggle nearly as much as the blowjob itself.

So I wrapped one fist around his base, and a second just above it, and relaxed.

I could *almost* swallow his entire dick this way.

I rolled the hands in opposite directions from one another and slowly filled my mouth.

His groans suddenly grew into panting. What happened next unfolded very quickly.

Mr. Brig wrapped his hands firmly around mine, then quickly but softly rolled me onto my back. My hands were still on his dick, and his dick was still in my mouth.

I worked faster, because I knew what was about to come.

I had learned to aim for the back of my throat.

He was pumping into me at this point, too overwhelmed with the moment to appreciate how little my mouth was, but simply not caring.

His cumload confirmed that he had been waiting a week. I tried to swallow during the thrusts, but he was working my jaw too hard for me to control any part of my mouth. I felt like I was drinking from a firehouse.

Inevitably, I overflowed.

He let out a soft groan as he saw how much was spilling out. Then he pulled his dick out entirely, wrapped one of his hands around two of mine, and used my hands as a masturbation tool while he finished.

All over my face. And eyes, nose, neck, and ears.

I had always assumed that finishing on a woman's face was dirty and vulgar.

It turns out that I was right.

But that's the reason I liked it. *Everything* about fucking each other is base, human, *extremely* vulnerable, and potentially awful. The *intensity* of the outcome, and not the guarantee of it, is the thrill that drives every lustful person. The facial could have been disgusting or demeaning, but the same is true about being spanked, choked, or fucked. I opened myself to the *possibility* of being made vulgar by the one person who held more power over me than any other.

So I swallowed what was left in my mouth.

And he bent down to kiss me.

He had risen to watch the sunrise, and I had followed to prolong our time together. He sat on one of the balcony's chairs, wrapped in the blanket. I was nestled in the fetal position on his lap, almost entirely covered by his blanket, my head resting on his chest. I occasionally stroked my fingernails up and down his shaft, which was snugly pressed between our torsos. I don't know how long I lingered in the gray, hazy warmth between asleep and awake, but I knew I didn't want it to end.

"Mr. Brig, do you have to work? Do I have to go to school? Can we just stay here, relaxing in this chair, watching the sun rise forever?"

He kissed the top of my head. "No, Lily," he responded softly in his chocolaty voice. "And I wouldn't want to, even if it were possible."

I made a pouty face, then felt silly when I realized that he couldn't see it. "Why don't you want to stay with me?"

He slipped a hand under the blanket and interlocked his fingers with mine. "I want to stay with you, Lily. I just don't want to stay *here* with you."

I pulled back the blanket and peeked my head out into the cool morning air. "What's wrong with right here?"

He looked down at me and raised an eyebrow. "Lily, we've driven each other crazy by *being* crazy for each other.

After everything we've gone through, don't you want the exciting part?"

I raised a sleepy head and kissed his lips softly. "Being with you has been the most exciting part of my life," I explained dreamily.

He smiled. "You're feeling everything for the first time. You may not realize it, but *real* intimacy only exists between two people who have been with each other for a long while."

I smiled and nuzzled up against his neck. "Well, you can be very proud of yourself, Mr. Brig. What you did to me was *way* beyond any intimacy I ever expected to feel."

He laughed. Hard.

I looked up at him in apprehension. "Why are you laughing at me, Mr. Brig?"

He bent down and kissed me, firmer than before, and stroked my cheek. "Lily, it's been long time since I met a woman who was too much for me to handle. I *think* I can handle you, but you're a never-ending source of surprises." He stared at me deeply, and my world felt like it was spinning. I turned away.

He reached a finger to my chin and pulled my head back around. "But *if* I can handle you, and *if* you can handle me..."

I reached up to kiss him, then ducked away before he could pull me in too deeply.

"...let's just say that, for my appetite, you're still a virgin."

Book Three: Between her Rock and his Hard Place

Chapter One

"NO!" I screamed, grabbing my phone from Carmen's hand and tumbling to the floor.

But it was too late.

"Damn, girl, you were *not* lying about his girth!"

I buried my face in my hands, curling into the fetal position. "I *told* you not to scroll through my photos so fast, Carmen!"

"Yeah," she said, and I could hear the grin in her voice, "but you didn't tell me that you were hiding dirty pics *right* next to all those *cute* images of the labradoodle you saw outside of class."

"It looked cute, and I wanted you to see it," I mumbled through my fingers.

"It *was* cute. Thick, too."

I playfully slapped her shin.

Then she knelt down, pulled my hands away from my face, and held them gently. "Get up, Lily. There's no reason to be embarrassed about being turned on by your own boyfriend."

I looked up at her warily. "You don't think I'm dirty for carrying those pics around with me?"

She had a way of smiling so brightly that the entire room seemed to warm up. "Of course I think you're dirty, just like the rest of us." She pulled me into a standing position. "And that's what makes us happy, so we should embrace it."

I tried to turn away, but she held my hands firmly in place. I slowly turned back to face her.

"So," she asked coyly, her fingertips dancing in mine, "is it just the one dick pic, or is there more to see?"

I pulled my hands away and plopped back down on her bed. "How'd you end up with a single room again?"

She sat down next to me once more. "My would-be roommate declined admission one day before freshman orientation, there was an odd number of students, they told me that I'd be the first to get a new roommate if something changed, and I think they forgot about it." She shrugged. "I'm not going to ask any questions. But you're only prodding out of embarrassment that I saw what your boyfriends *thick, meaty, cock* looked like, and you want to change the topic." She playfully jabbed my ribs at these last few words, and I playfully resisted. "Besides, you like it." She stared at me purposefully, and I calmly met her gaze.

"How do you know that?" I asked meekly.

She shrugged. "Because if you *didn't*, you would have said so. But asking *how* I know implies that I was right in my assumption. You like thinking and talking about Mr. Brig, and after I saw him last week, I understood why." She stroked my finger.

I wanted to hide my face again. "I feel like such a freak sometimes. I mean, the oldest students on campus are half his age."

"And half his *je ne sais quoi*. You have no reason to deny that, Lily," she pressed, still smiling. "You like talking about him, but you feel guilty about your sexuality. So you pretend to hate it out of self-preservation, then expect me to chase you down for the details. It leaves you feeling guiltless and interesting at the same time."

I tried to form a response, said nothing, then giggled at myself. Then I pulled one of her pillows close, hid half of my face, and peeked out from over its edge. "How do you figure things out so well?"

She brushed a lock of my hair aside. "Lily, I really know women."

I sobbed uncontrollably on the car ride. The terrified-looking Uber driver didn't say a word, and I know he was happy to see me finally tumble out the door.

I rushed into the Reagan UCLA entrance and struggled to form words for the receptionist.

Finally, I got a room number and directions.

Then I waited, alone, next to other crying families.

After ten minutes, my fingers stopped shaking long enough for me to use a phone.

"It will be okay, Lily. I promise. Tell me that you believe me."

Mr. Brig's words had an immediate calming effect on me, but I was still shaken. "I don't know what to believe. All I know is that Mom was in a bad accident-"

"Lily, it will be fine. You know that I love both you and your mom, and I'll be there as soon as I can."

I sniffed. "You promise?"

"Yes, I promise. This business meeting can't happen without me, so they're going to have to adjust to my terms."

Despite the intensity of the moment – or perhaps because of it – a thrill of adrenaline rose in my chest as I understood how powerful Mr. Brig really was. "How long will it take for you to get back?"

He shuffled the phone around. "I have my secretary looking into flights right now, but there's nothing available until local time in the morning. The flight from Tokyo to LA is about ten hours, so it will be at least a day. I'm so sorry, Lily. I love you, and I promise that I'll be there as soon as I can."

I sniffed. "And I feel the same as I always have."

A nurse interrupted me. "Lily? Your mom is ready to see you."

I had been in such a hurry to get inside the hospital that I never considered just how terrified I would be to enter the room. I suddenly wanted to be anywhere but where I was.

I placed my hand on the knob and opened the door.

I gasped.

Mom was injured but awake. She smiled meekly at me. "Hey there, Lilliput."

One arm and one leg were both in casts, but her face was untouched. I had been terrified that she would be much worse. I raced over to hug her.

"Oof, careful. I'm very fragile right now."

I drew back and wiped my eyes. "I'm sorry Mom, it's just – I was *so scared*." I wiped my eyes. "A lot of memories about losing Dad came back, and-"

I couldn't go on. She squeezed my hand. "I know, Lily, I know," she explained softly. She took a deep breath. "Did you talk to – um, Harrison?"

My stomach clenched. It was still an awkward topic between us, even if she had conceded a quiet acceptance of our relationship. "Yeah. He's on his way over to see you."

She nodded quietly. "Where's he coming from?"

I sighed. "Japan."

She laughed meekly. "That man always would jump over oceans for the things he loved."

A heavy paused hung between us.

I cleared my throat. "I'm sorry that things ended between you and Annalise. This a rotten time to feel alone."

She raised an eyebrow. "Well, Lily, life has a funny way of throwing things at you when you're least prepared."

Carmen wrapped her arms around me, and I buried my face in her neck. Wordlessly, she stroked my hair.

Then she took me by the hand and led me into her room. She sat on the edge of the bed, and waited for me to talk.

I breathed a little easier. "I… don't even know how to process what I'm feeling. I'm still terrified for my mom's health, relieved that she's going to be okay, angry that I got so scared, guilty that I'm feeling relieved, *also* guilty for feeling angry, stupid for making Harrison fly home, excited that I'm going to see him, depressed at the memory of my dad's death, and frustrated that I feel so dramatic over everything." I sighed. "It's like all my emotions are at war with each other. I don't know what to do."

She hugged me, kissed my forehead, and leaned against me.

We stayed like that for some time, doing nothing.

I felt significantly better.

"I don't want to go back to my room. What if I start crying again? Emma already thinks I'm crazy."

Carmen smiled. "She knows that, but doesn't appreciate it? She's nuts."

I grinned despite myself.

She squeezed my shoulder. "Just stay the night here. This is no time to be alone. You'll feel better in the morning."

I wiped away a tear. "Thank you."

Despite everything, I couldn't help being envious of her single room. We were able to go about the process of getting ready for bed without the feeling of intrusion.

It was very liberating.

"Okay, let's get some rest," Carmen said soothingly as she clicked off one of the lights.

Then she turned around and slid her shorts over her feet, kicking them aside. Next, she pulled her t-shirt over her head and dropped that to the floor. Then she casually reached behind her back, unclasped her bra, and slid it off her arms.

She stood before me wearing nothing but panties.

I don't know why I was so focused on the sight before of me. The perfect roundness of her nipples was mesmerizing; it echoed the complete rotundity of her breasts. Their shape had been apparent beneath her shirt, but seeing them free provided much more detail than I had ever considered.

"I said, what are you looking at?"

I snapped my attention back to her face. She looked half-perplexed, half-amused. "Come on, you need some sleep."

I nodded in confusion.

Then I looked down at my own body in *further* confusion.

What should I wear to bed? I preferred sleeping bottomless, but that was clearly unreasonable. Instead, I slipped my arms inside my shirt, unhooked my bra, and pulled it free without any risk of exposing my own breasts. I slid my shorts down, taking great care to leave my panties firmly in place. This kept my lower regions protected by both my underwear and the bottom part of my shirt.

She crawled into her bed, then lifted the blanket invitingly. I delicately climbed in after her.

It was very warm.

She clicked off the lamp, and waves of relaxation overcame me as the heat from her body contrasted with the cool sheets. I'd only ever shared a bed with Mr. Brig, and this felt very different.

I turned away from her and pulled the blanket under my chin. She wrapped an arm around me, turning me into the little spoon. It was extremely comforting; the front of her thighs pressed softly into the backs of mine, our bare feet rubbed against each other, and the feeling of loneliness melted into comforting sleep.

The only unusual sensation was her bare breasts pushed firmly against my back.

I woke up so relaxed that it took several seconds to remember the trauma of the night before.

The feelings hit me all at once.

Fear. Relief. Frustration.

Excitement that Mr. Brig was coming home. Guilt that he cancelled his trip for nothing.

And then I thought about the fact that one day, it *would* be something. We spend our lives in a state of assumed immortality, only able to live with the inevitability of death because we don't believe it. The years had a way of going faster and faster, and the reality is that most of my mom's life was probably behind her.

One day, I *would* be alone.

The dam finally broke then, and I was powerless to stop the tears. They did not arrive in great, heaving sobs; instead they came out slowly and delicately, pouring down my face in a calm but relentless torrent that proved just how weak I was beneath their force.

"Hey. Hey, what's wrong?" Carmen asked soothingly. She propped herself up on one elbow, reaching her hand around and wiping my eyes. The action caused her breasts to swing with a casual beauty that I was unable to categorize.

I welcomed her caress on my face, and I welcomed the hug that followed.

Warmth that flows from skin-to-skin contact has an entirely different caliber from any other, and its most distinctive characteristic is that it cannot be explained.

I reached back and pulled her close, not realizing how *desperately* I needed to be hugged in that overwhelming moment, and completely unaware of the kiss until we were deep into it. There was no thought, consideration, or explanation – just her lips against mine, our tongues lightly dancing with each other, and warmth. Imagine a dying person finally emerging from a desert that had seemed endless. If there were a glass of water, he would drink without thought, having *finally* found the greatest thing he didn't know he was missing until it seemed lost forever. I *needed* loving contact like I needed air, and I threw myself into the kiss with such an overwhelming hunger that I nearly cried.

I pulled back. Her eyes were closed, and she was smiling.

Shock, warmth, guilt, joy, and an overwhelming sense of *wrongness* curdled in my stomach.

The only thing I knew in that moment is that I had to leave.

Everything seemed wrong. Where was my shirt? I was wearing it. Those weren't my shorts, they were hers. *I shouldn't be picking up my pants from another person's floor.* Why could I find my shoes, but not my socks? Had I worn socks?

I fucked up.

"Lily, wait," Carmen said, getting out of bed.

I knew that I couldn't look at her chest. Not again. That would just make things worse.

"I have to go, Carmen. I have to go." I *thought* that I had put all my clothes back on, but in my daze, I wasn't sure.

"Lily!" she called, grabbing me with one hand. The other was holding the blanket around her breasts.

I stared at her, expecting an explanation.

But for once, she had none.

The first wave of nausea hit, and I broke away from her grasp.

I ran out the door, knowing that she had to stay behind if she didn't want the world to see her nakedness.

I visited Mom in her room that morning. She was doing much better.

"Harrison should be here in an hour. Do you want to wait for him?"

I struggled to find the words, but found none. She took my hand, smiled sadly, and returned my silence.

Moms always know.

I waited nervously outside of his apartment building for him to return from the hospital. The anticipation was so unbearable that I just wanted it to be over with.

But when I saw his Jaguar pull up, I wanted to be anywhere on earth but there.

He could tell that something was wrong right away, but waited until we were in his living room before prying.

Even in that moment, his only pressure was to sit quietly and give me space to talk.

It was one of the million reasons why he was the best man I'd ever known.

I had turned over the explanation in my head more times than I could count, and the only result it produced was a mental spaghetti of disjointed words and sentence fragments. I didn't even understand *what* I was feeling; putting those feelings into language seemed beyond impossible.

Finally, I opened my mouth, and the words tumbled out. "I kissed someone."

Agonizing as it was, it felt good to finally be free of the ugliness inside me.

Mr. Brig's face turned ashen, and he moved very stiffly. I wanted him to say something, *anything*, but he remained brutally silent.

"I – I didn't mean to, I promise, I promise! I've been *unable* to stop thinking about the fact that I might have just destroyed the most important thing I have, that I've deeply hurt the man I love more than I love myself, and that the rest of my life will be spent chasing the uncatchable ghost of your memory if you leave me now." Tears flowed down my face, but neither of us wiped them away. The thought of Carmen's gentle caress arose involuntarily. "Please tell me that we can make it okay, Mr. Brig." I felt ready to shatter at the slightest touch.

He didn't reject me, but he didn't comfort me, either. "Lily," he spoke in a voice that conveyed disappointment, but not anger, "I'm having a hard time understanding how you *accidentally* kissed someone."

"I don't know," I wailed, "and I realize that *saying* I don't know makes no sense. I was more terrified of my mom's accident than even *I* realized, I felt so helpless and alone, and she was just so *comforting* that I-"

"Wait," Mr. Brig interjected, a strange look on his face. "*She?*"

I nodded. "It's – it's all just so complicated. I didn't even know I'd want to kiss her, or *any* girl for that matter, which is why it all caught me off guard, and-"

"Well," he continued, seeming genuinely interested, "how was it that you to were even in a *position* to kiss each other?"

I shrugged. "We were in bed together."

His breathing quickened.

"I – I mean, I thought it was just as friends. I guess there were warning signs, but I didn't realize what they were at the time. I feel stupid."

He hugged me, and the same sudden relief that I'd felt in Carmen's bed washed over me.

"Do you hate me, Mr. Brig?"

He pulled back and wiped my tears. "Never."

He kissed me then, and it was a strong contender for the best one I'd had that day.

When he finished, I felt healed – at least partially.

"So you've never had any experience with a girl before this?" he asked.

He sounded almost eager.

I clutched his hand. "Harrison, I've been through an emotional roller coaster over the past couple of days. It would mean the world if I could open up to you, but I need to know that we're okay first."

He hugged me close and kissed the top of my head. "I'm yours, you're mine, and we're safe," he whispered.

I took his hand in mine, and we slid our fingers together. "Can you take me into your room so that we can talk?"

He lifted me wordlessly, then walked with me across the apartment like I was a bride being carried over the threshold. I wrapped my arms around his neck, and we looked at nothing but each other as he moved.

When we got to his room, he set me down on the floor. Wordlessly, he undressed me until I stood naked in front of him. I felt small, but safe.

Then I quietly and methodically unbuttoned his shirt, unzipped his pants, folded his clothes, and put them away.

We took each other's hands and crawled into bed. I turned away from him, and he embraced me as the little spoon. His erection fit warmly between my cheeks.

"Tell me what you've been feeling, Lily," he said with comforting authority, taking my small hand in his large one.

I talked. As I opened up more, I could feel myself melting into his contours, our bodies becoming molded to each other until we had re-shaped ourselves to fit together in a way that had once seemed impossible.

"I've only ever wanted men, Harrison. Well, to be honest, I've only ever wanted *you*. I've never really considered any desire for other people."

He squirmed slightly. "You've never felt a base attraction? Never wanted to watch porn?"

There was a time when I would have felt embarrassed. But I felt so open, naked, and raw in this moment that I was ready to discuss things that I'd hidden even from myself. "Yes, I've seen it a couple of times, and... yeah, it was fun." I squirmed as well. "But when I'm touching myself, I want to imagine someone I *know*, not an anonymous actor."

He kissed my cheek.

"So I guess I've never really thought about anyone else, because it's never been presented to me."

He stroked my hair. "So when you did watch porn, who did you like looking at? The men or the women?"

I shrugged. "Both. They were all beautiful, and I liked seeing them naked. Isn't that what everyone wants to see?"

He hugged me tightly. "There is no 'everyone' in sex, Lily. Just a limitless group of individuals looking to end their loneliness, even for just a moment." He rolled his fingers over my knuckles. "So tell me about this kiss."

Tears fell suddenly and without warning. "Do you promise that you're not mad?"

He leaned in and kissed me again. "I'll only be upset if you hold back who you are."

I looked into his eyes, and was overwhelmed with such a firm feeling of safety that I suddenly couldn't remember what my concerns were. "You met Carmen when you came to the dining hall last week, remember?"

He raised an eyebrow. "The hot one?"

I smiled sheepishly. "I mean, I suppose. Guys won't stop hitting on her."

"And girls, from what I understand."

I buried my face in my hand. "Anyway. She invited me to sleep over at her place on the night of the accident, and I didn't want to be alone, so-"

"What did she wear?"

"What?"

"What did she wear to bed, Lily?"

"Um, pink panties."

"No top?"

"No, she was topless."

His erection suddenly pressed against my ass. It thrilled me to feel it nestled against my body as though it belonged there. I pushed back, stroking it gently, and he whimpered.

"You're telling me that you didn't know what she was doing?"

I reached my arm behind my head, running my fingers through his hair. "I suppose I decided not to think about it." I grabbed his locks firmly, knowing that my grip bordered on causing him pain. "She spooned me, just like you are right now."

I could no longer ignore the amount of precum on my back. My gentle rubbing had coated my ass and his dick in his own fluids, and they now slid against each other with ease.

"Her thighs were so soft, Harrison. You'd have loved them." His sliding increased, and I couldn't stop the smile from spreading across my face. "And you should see her breasts, Mr. Brig. I know how much you love the feeling of nipples between your teeth, and hers are just begging to be tasted." I pulled his hair well past the point of pain as he bit down on my shoulder.

"Show me how she kissed you," he gasped.

I looked up at him. "Her face was right where yours is now."

This one *was* the best kiss of the day. His lips found mine in the same moment that he finally penetrated me. I *adored* the feeling of being filled from both ends, like he needed to consume me whole and could not get enough all at once. It overwhelmed me, and I loved the loss of control.

Harrison was *very* talented at fucking in the spooning position. His slender hips belied the amount of muscle in his sinewy abs and thighs, but it became apparent just how much power he could generate when his waist was hitting mine from behind. The position caused our inner thighs and asses to be soaking wet, and the baseness was part of what I loved about it.

His length, girth, and power still frightened me, to be sure.

But I loved the fear.

So I decided to pour some gasoline on the fire.

"You wish you could have seen us kiss, don't you, Mr. Brig?"

He pumped faster.

"Her lips were so soft."

Faster. It was getting hard to talk.

"I could feel-" *gasp* "feel" *gasp* "feel her nipples through my t-shirt-"

He was now impaling me too ferociously for me to speak.

Or even breathe.

The brink of unconsciousness drifted hazily forward as he split me open with an intensity that was, quite simply, too much for me to handle.

Then he groaned so loudly that he was nearly yelling.

The wetness in my crotch now included an overflow of cum. He pulled out of me, lifted one thigh with his left hand, and jerked himself off with his right.

He was still cumming.

I looked down as he shot rope after rope onto my most vulnerable places. As I watched, he covered my clit, pussy lips, pubic hair, and inner thigh with a shocking flood of cum.

When he was finished, I couldn't even see my own lips or clit beneath the flood he had left on me.

He kissed my ear. "Masturbate for me, Lily."

I obeyed immediately.

The sensation was very odd at first. While fluid helps masturbation, the sheer quantity was overwhelming.

"Make a mess," he breathed.

That made things easier.

I sank my fingers deeply into his spunk, massaging it into my pussy, wiping it across my clit, and letting it squish playfully between my fingers. I embraced the dirtiness of it, spreading his cum all over my body and relishing the feeling.

I pressed my right middle finger into my pussy, stuffing a fingerfull of hot jizz inside of me. I scooped up a healthy serving with my left hand, then wiped it onto my tongue and licked my fingers like it was cake frosting.

It was an acquired tasted that I loved acquiring. As it slid down my throat, I smeared a sizable dollop on my clit, spreading it furiously as I rubbed myself clockwise. A squishing, slurping sound filled my ears, sending me close to the edge, and I gasped every time my fingertips came around to the twelve o'clock position.

Mr. Brig scooped up some of his own cum, then reached around me. At first, I was confused.

A rocket went off in my head as I felt him spread the cum onto my asshole.

There was no *approaching* the edge; I was instantly cumming. My body attempted to process the feelings of my finger on my clit, Mr. Brig's finger on my asshole, the taste in my mouth, and the knowledge that he had absolutely covered me in his cum. I couldn't focus on a single thing at once, and I closed my eyes as the confusing sensations overwhelmed me. I embraced the feeling; instead of trying to figure out *what* was going on inside my own head, I simply welcomed it unabashedly as it washed over my being.

I came down from the orgasm gradually, Mr. Brig offering soft butterfly kisses along the way.

"Do you want to take a shower break?" he asked.

I closed my eyes and smiled. "Mr. Brig, your cum is *everywhere*." I sighed contentedly. "I'd like to leave it there for a while."

I dozed on and off, loving the sensation of re-discovering his cum coating every time I woke up.

Finally, it seemed right to speak again. "I'm feeling much better now, but I'm still very, very confused."

He kissed my cheek. "Welcome to enlightenment."

I furrowed my brow. "But why did I like kissing Carmen? I thought I only liked men."

"But you've enjoyed seeing naked women."

I shrugged. "Doesn't everyone?"

"Everyone who's attracted to women." He kissed my bare shoulder.

"But how can I be a lesbian? I'm in love with you, Mr. Brig."

He laughed. "Lily, it just sounds like you're bi-curious. Have you heard of the Kinsey Scale?"

I shook my head.

"Basically, it means that sexual orientation can be hard to pin down for some people. The solid definition *is* that there's no solid definition, and it means that the answer to your questions is to question."

A flash of worry ran through my chest. "And you're okay with me – you know – questioning?"

He gently raked my arm with his fingernails, sending goosebumps across my body. "You're not questioning your love for me, are you?"

I laughed aloud. "No, Mr. Brig." I kissed his cheek. "That's rock-hard."

"Okay, then," he sighed. "You're eighteen, which means you have a *lot* to learn about yourself. Believe me, it's been a mental adjustment on my end. But," he pressed, moving his head above my own, "one of the things I promised myself is that I wouldn't get in the way of you being you. These are the things that you have to discover about yourself. The process of finding out *is* the process of living, not some unfortunate side effect. As long as we establish some ground rules and boundaries, I want you to seek answers to your questions."

I looked up at him in complete adoration and slowly stroked his cheek. "And how do I do that, Mr. Brig?"

He looked down at me with a deep hunger that sent a chill through my spine and into my toes.

"You need to have sex with your friend Carmen."

How to read the next part

Caressa Pink is the author of the *Daddy's Taboo Secrets* series, all of which is available through Amazon. You can read previews at www.reddit.com/r/BitesofDesire.